D0571131

For Elise, Olívia, and Leo— wishing you happy playtimes, full of friends
—G. S.

For Bella, with love
—A. C.

First published in Great Britain in June 2017 by Bloomsbury Publishing Plc
Published in the United States of America in February 2018
by Bloomsbury Children's Books
www.bloomsbury.com

Bloomsbury is a registered trademark of Bloomsbury Publishing Plc

For information about permission to reproduce selections from this book, write to
Permissions, Bloomsbury Children's Books, 1385 Broadway, New York, New York 10018
Bloomsbury books may be purchased for business or promotional use. For information on bulk purchases
please contact Macmillan Corporate and Premium Sales Department at specialmarkets@macmillan.com

Library of Congress Cataloging-in-Publication Data
Names: Shields, Gillian, author. | Currey, Anna, illustrator.
Title: When the world is full of friends / by Gillian Shields ; illustrated by Anna Currey.
Description: New York : Bloomsbury, 2018.
Summary: Four young rabbit siblings use their unique talents to devise a way to cross the stream and make friends with the squirrels who just moved there.
Identifiers: LCCN 2017020809 (print) | LCCN 2017037300 (e-book)
ISBN 978-1-68119-626-8 (hardcover)
ISBN 978-1-68119-840-8 (e-book) • ISBN 978-1-68119-841-5 (e-PDF)
Subjects: | CYAC: Friendship—Fiction. | Individuality—Fiction. | Rabbits—Fiction. | Squirrels—Fiction.
Classification: LCC PZ7.S55478 Whe 2018 (print) | LCC PZ7.S55478 (e-book) | DDC [E]—dc23
LC record available at https://lccn.loc.gov/2017020809

Art created with pen and ink and watercolor • Typeset in Lorelei and Truesdell • Book design by Zoe Waring
Printed in China by Leo Paper Products, Heshan, Guangdong
2 4 6 8 10 9 7 5 3 1

All papers used by Bloomsbury Publishing, Inc., are natural, recyclable products made from wood grown in well-managed forests.
The manufacturing processes conform to the environmental regulations of the country of origin.

When the World Is Full of Friends

Gillian Shields
illustrated by Anna Currey

BLOOMSBURY
NEW YORK LONDON OXFORD NEW DELHI SYDNEY

When the world
Is ready to play,
Friends are near
If you find a way . . .

Everyone in the Rabbit family loved to play.

Albert loved to run and hop and jump.

He was the fastest and strongest in all the little rabbits' races and games.

Tom liked stories and dressing up best.

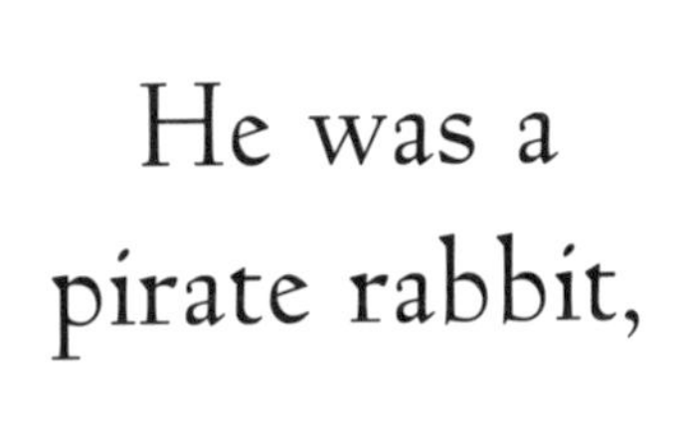

He was a
pirate rabbit,

a monster
rabbit,

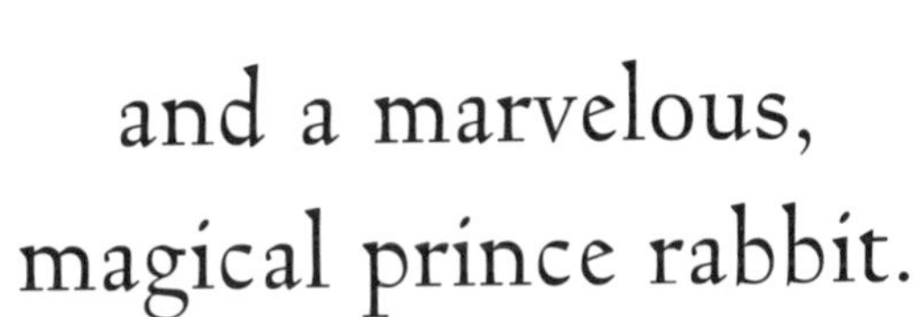

and a marvelous,
magical prince rabbit.

Flossie was a great inventor.

She loved to make things and paint them bright colors—windmills and forts and twirly paper umbrellas.

As for the baby, Pipkin—he loved best of all
to play on his blankie by the wide, watery stream,
catching his toes in the sunshine.

So the little rabbits played together,
and they were busy and good.

One day, though, when they were all rather tired,
Flossie said, "I wish we had some friends to play with."
"Friends!" said Albert.
"Friends!" said Tom.
"Ooh!" squeaked Pipkin.

And they knew that they wanted friends
more than anything else in the world.

The very next morning, something truly wonderful happened. A family of squirrels came to live on the other side of the stream, and there were two small squirrels—just the right size to be friends.

The little rabbits and squirrels waved to one another.

“Now we’ll have friends
to play with!” cried Flossie.
But it wasn’t as simple as that . . .

"How can we get across the wide, watery stream?" asked Albert.
"There isn't a bridge for miles!"

"Oh, no!" said Tom.
"Ooh!" squeaked Pipkin.
It was so very disappointing.

But Flossie knew there must be a way.
She sat quietly and tried to figure it out.

"I'll think of something—I've got to!"

Then Flossie had an amazing idea.
"We'll tie balloons to a basket
and fly across the stream,"
she explained.

Oh dear! The balloons
weren't big or airy enough
to make the basket fly.

"We could hop, skip,
and leap across!" said Albert.
"I don't think so," said Mother Rabbit, kindly.
Even Albert couldn't leap that far.
The little rabbits and squirrels felt so sad.

But Flossie wouldn't give up.
She invented and invented,
until at last she said,
"Albert, you're fast and strong.
Run and find some nice
big pieces of wood and rope."

So Albert did, and when Father Rabbit saw what the little rabbits were trying to make he smiled and came to help . . .

. . . until their brave,
beautiful boat was finished.

"We must dress up!" said Tom.
Soon the little rabbits looked
like daring sailors and pirates,
ready for the voyage.

There was only one more thing they needed.

"A sail," explained Flossie.
"Blankie!" squeaked Pipkin.
And it made the perfect sail!

"Jump aboard, sailors,"
said Father Rabbit
with a laugh.

He steered them safely across the wide, watery stream,
where they met the little squirrels at last.

"Hooray!" they all shouted. "Now we can be friends!"
"Hoo-hoo!" squeaked Pipkin.
And Flossie was right . . .

Playing with friends
was wonderful!

When the world
Is full of friends,
The fun and laughter
Never ends.